Jessica's Two Families

Helping Children Learn to Cope with Blended Households

By
Lynne Hugo, LPCC

Illustrations by
Adam Gordon

New Horizon Press
Far Hills, New Jersey

For Ciera, star of classroom, stage, soccer field,
volleyball court and my heart.

New Horizon Press
P.O. Box 669
Far Hills, NJ 07931

Lynne Hugo
     Jessica's Two Families: Helping Children Learn to Cope with Blended Households

Cover Design: Norma Ehrler Rahn
Interior Design: Catherine Finegan

Library of Congress Control Number: 2004118084

ISBN: 0-88282-263-2
SMALL HORIZONS
A Division of New Horizon Press

2009   2008   2007   2006   2005   /   5   4   3   2   1

Printed in Hong Kong

Daddy always tells how pruny and red I was the day I was born. I wailed up a storm, louder than any other baby! He put his State Champions baseball cap on me because I was the best crier in the hospital.

We all seemed to stick together like peanut butter and jelly. Then my parents said they were getting a divorce. I was very mad and very sad. I became the champion crier in the *world*.

Mommy was the first parent to get married again. I wore a floppy hat and a blue princess dress when I was a flower girl in her wedding to Mike, my stepfather.

I did not want another daddy. I wanted my own daddy back. Now I only get to see Daddy on the weekends.

I look just like my daddy. Our big brown eyes are exactly the same. We have the same dimple on our left ears. Sometimes I felt very mad at my dad for moving away, though.

One Saturday when Daddy came to pick me up, he and Mom fought about me. They thought I couldn't hear them. I did. I hid in the closet. Mommy found me.

"I don't want to go anywhere!" I pouted. "I don't want to come to your house!" I yelled at Daddy.

"Jess, don't say that," he said. "I love you."

My stomach hurt then.

Sometimes I really did want to go, a lot. Dad makes great spaghetti and meatballs. He even got us a dog, a cuddly beagle. I named him Copper.

Daddy gave me a ball and bat, too. "Maybe you can join a team, like me," he said. We went outside to practice. Daddy swung his arm like a pinwheel to wind up really funny. "Watch the ball," he said.

THWACK! The ball hopped like a really fast rabbit. Daddy's mouth made a giant O. "GREAT HIT!!" he shouted.

THWACK! My next hit zoomed like a white rocket over his head.

"WOW!" he yelled.

Before dinner, Daddy gave me his special State Champions hat. I kept it on while we ate spaghetti.

I hid the special hat when Daddy took me home to Mommy's and Mike's.

"Look how pink your cheeks are!" Mommy said.

"What did you do with your dad?" Mike asked.

"Oh, nothing," I said. I didn't want Mommy to think I didn't want to be with her.

The next weekend I was excited to go to Daddy's and hit balls again. I planned to wear my Champions hat. INSTEAD…

"Jessica, there is somebody I want you to meet," Daddy said when Mommy dropped me off at his house and I went inside. "This is my friend Beth and these are Beth's children, Megan and Ryan. Megan is almost eight, so she is just a year older than you. Ryan is five."

"All of us are going to the zoo this afternoon."

While we were there, I saw Daddy hold Beth's hand. Even though my ice cream cone was double chocolate, I felt like feeding it to the nearest monkey.

"Let's do something with them again next weekend," Daddy said when he took me home later. "It will be fun."

"What about our baseball?" I asked.

"GREAT idea, honey. We can all play baseball if the weather is good."

I didn't tell him that was *not* what I wanted. I wanted it to be just Daddy and me.

Pretty soon Daddy and Beth got married. Megan and I were flower girls. We wore matching dresses that looked like cotton candy, but felt like sandpaper.

I was the crying champion of the universe after that wedding. I was sad and mad all the time.

Dad moved to Beth's house. That meant I had to go to Beth's house to visit him on weekends. They put another bed in Megan's room. Beth said, "Jessica, this is your room now, too."

Megan did not want to share her room with me. She took a piece of chalk and drew a line down the middle of the room. "Stay on your side," she said in a mean voice.

Megan even got Copper to come into her side of the room!

"He belongs over here. Copper is my dog!" I said.

"No, he can be on either side. Copper is the family dog," Megan said. She kind of yelled, but not too loudly.

"He is *mine*. My dad got him for *me*!" I was loud.

I heard Beth coming upstairs. "You're in trouble now," Megan said.

Beth opened the bedroom door. "Jessica, we do not allow yelling in our family," she said, sounding strict. "This is a warning. Next time there will be a punishment." Then she went back downstairs. Megan went with her.

I hugged Copper and looked outside Megan's bedroom window. My daddy was outside playing baseball with Ryan! I had packed my special baseball cap so my dad would play baseball with *me* today. Daddy waved to me to come out, but I did not. I threw myself on the bed like a big rag doll and cried.

Finally, Daddy came inside. "Honey, you look all pruny and red," he said. "Have you been crying again? What's the matter?"

I sniffled. "I want to go home."

"Jess, you are supposed to spend the night here. We are having a campfire. Are you sure you want to go?"

I started to cry more. Daddy sighed and called my mom.

When I got to my other house, I was happy to see Mommy. I thought we could snuggle on the couch and watch a movie. Then Mike said, "Jessica, your mother and I made plans to go out alone tonight. Your favorite babysitter can come, though."

"What?! I came home to be with my mother!" I was so mad I screamed and stamped my feet.

"Jessica, I will not stand for a tantrum! Go to your room," said Mike.

Mommy said, "Jessica, Mike is right. You need to go to your room. You may come out when you calm down."

In the morning I pretended to be sick. I did not want to go to school. "You do not have a fever," Mom said. She drove me to school and talked with my teacher, Mrs. Tuttle, before class.

After the bell rang, Mrs. Tuttle said, "Today we are going to talk about families." She asked how many people had two families. Five children raised their hands.

"Lots of people have two families," she said. "There are tough times, but there is a lot of good, too. It helps to talk about your feelings. I have two families. It took time for me to figure out that I had a place in each one." I just stared at the shiny silver buttons on her jumper. Maybe she did not know that no one cared about me anymore except a dog. I didn't even get to be with Copper very much.

When I got off the bus that afternoon, my mom and my dad were waiting for me. *Hurray*, I thought. *They are getting back together!*

No such luck. We all went inside the house and sat in the living room.

"Honey, we are worried about you. Even though we are each married to other people now, the two of us are still your parents. We both love you. We do not want you to be unhappy," Daddy said.

"Then marry each other again," I begged.

"We cannot do that, Jess," Mommy said.

"Why not?"

"Because we were not able to keep loving each other," she answered.

"Then maybe you cannot love me anymore, either." I said.

"Honey, that would never happen," Daddy said.

"Jessica," said Mommy, "we made an appointment with a family counselor to help us all get along together."

"What is a counselor?" I asked, scrunching up my face.

"A counselor talks to people about their problems and how to fix them," Daddy told me.

I was scared to go at first.

Mommy and Mike took me to my first visit. A friendly woman came out to meet us in the waiting room.

"I'm Brooke, your family counselor," she said. She smiled. "Are you Jessica?" she asked. I nodded. My mouth felt stuffed with cotton balls.

When we were in her office, Brooke slid her chair over next to mine. "Don't worry. This is a safe place to talk about feelings," she said. She asked if I had any pets. She said her dog steals her food if she is not watching! We both laughed. I wasn't so scared anymore.

After a little while, Brooke called Mommy and Mike into her office.

"How does having two families seem to you, Jess?" Brooke asked.

"I don't like it." I told Brooke how confusing it all was. "There are too many different rules. I have to share my mom and dad." I kept thinking of bad things.

Brooke said, "Jessica, many kids whose parents remarry feel upset. There are lots more people around. Yet the kids feel lonely."

Then Brooke said, "Some kids also feel angry at their parents. Do you ever feel that way?"

"Sort of," I whispered.

"Have you felt angry with your mom?"

I squirmed like a worm in my chair and looked down. "Mommy likes Mike best now. She used to do more with just me before she married him." I started crying hard, like my eyes were raining on my face. Brooke handed me a tissue.

"Thanks for telling us, Jess! What did your mom used to do that you miss the most?" Brooke asked.

"She read me three stories before bed instead of just one," I said. "We would talk before I went to sleep. Now she just hurries downstairs to be with Mike."

"Great job, Jessica," Brooke said. "I bet that is the best you've ever done telling your mom how you feel."

"It sure is," Mom said. "It helps me to understand. I did not know that you were feeling lonely."

"You know, Jessica," Brooke said, "there are no perfect families. We need to figure out what is good in each of your families. We will work to make the good parts bigger."

"We also need to know what makes you sad or angry in each of your families. We will work together to make those parts smaller," she said. "Your two families are always going to be different from each other. That is okay. Next week, your dad, Beth, Megan and Ryan will come here with you. We will talk more about working together and being a family."

One week later, Daddy, Beth, Megan and Ryan all met in Brooke's office with me.

"Let's pick one problem you have in this family, Jessica. We'll talk about how to make it smaller," Brooke said.

I hung my head. "I don't want to hurt anyone's feelings."

"You can say whatever you feel in a calm voice," Brooke said. "It helps the whole family to understand."

I was scared, but I made myself say, "Megan doesn't like me in her room. It's all her stuff."

"How do you feel about that Megan?" Brooke asked.

"It used to be just my room. I liked that," Megan said. I could tell she felt bad and sort of mad, too, but her voice wasn't mean.

"Is there anything that would help you feel okay about sharing your room on the weekends?" Brooke asked.

Megan shrugged. Then she looked at her mom. "Maybe if we could redecorate it. I've always wanted a TV set in my room, too," she said.

"Good for you for giving an idea, Megan! How would the parents feel about that?" Brooke asked, turning to Daddy and Beth.

Beth answered, "We can rearrange the furniture the way you girls want. We could do it Saturday morning. Then we could go shopping. You two may pick out new quilts, new curtains and new posters for the walls. Would that plan work?"

That sounded pretty neat. "What's your favorite color?" I whispered to Megan.

"I like purple a lot!" Megan whispered.

"PURPLE is so cool!" I whispered back.

Daddy said, "I don't know about getting a television set. It would depend on your grades and how you two get along. We will talk about it some more. Does that seem fair?"

"I'd LIKE that." Megan's eyes got big. "Mom always said no way about a TV." Now Beth was nodding her head yes to what Daddy said.

"Jessica, I would like you to tell me something good about this family. We can make the good part BIGGER," Brooke said.

I thought and thought. "Daddy, could we have another campfire like the one I missed?"

The very next Saturday, Daddy and I played baseball, just us. After a while, Ryan joined the game. He can't THWACK the ball over Daddy's head the way I can, though. I wore my cap, of course.

When it got dark, Megan and Beth came outside. Daddy built a campfire. We all sang songs while we roasted marshmallows.

On Sunday I went back to my other house. Mommy and Mike and I spent a special night out. We all got dressed up like movie stars. Mommy put pink lipstick on my lips.

On Monday when I went to school, Mrs. Tuttle said, "Jessica, I am glad to see you wearing your Champions hat again. Have you found anything good about having two families yet?"

"Yes, I have," I said.

Mrs. Tuttle's smile was as shiny as her pretty buttons. "That makes me very happy, Jess," she said. "In two families there are more people to love and to love you back."

I smiled then, too. "I've learned that there's no such thing as too much love."

Tips for Kids

1. Remember that if your parents get a divorce, it is never your fault. Lots of kids wonder if they could have kept their parents together somehow. The answer is no.

2. It really helps to talk about what's going on inside of you when you are sad or mad. Some parents are great at listening and some are not as good at it. Try each of your parents first or a stepparent. If that does not work out, try a teacher or a counselor at school or your pediatrician or family doctor. You can also tell your mom or dad that you would like to talk to a family counselor.

3. You do not have to choose sides between your mom and dad. You can love them both. You do not have to pick which one to love most or which family you like being with most. You do not need to feel guilty at having a great time with either parent. It is NORMAL for a kid to love and want to be with both parents!

4. Remember that no family is perfect. When you are asked to help solve a problem at one of your homes, try to contribute an idea about how to make it better.

5. When a suggestion or an idea you try makes you feel better, be sure to let your parents know.

Tips for Parents

1. Keep in mind that any fighting between you and your former spouse during and after the divorce process is frightening and upsetting to your child. Whatever you can do to avoid friction will enhance his or her emotional well being.

2. Never use your child to carry messages to your former spouse.

3. It's helpful if the rules are not wildly different at each home. Obviously, some discrepancies will exist, but try to compromise to minimize them. If you cannot do this on your own, you might schedule an adult counseling session to negotiate rules to which both parents can agree.

4. Avoid negative comments about your child's other parent. While you were able to terminate your marital relationship, your child has a lifelong parent/child relationship to negotiate. Your child will also see him/herself as having inherited the genes of the other parent, so if you present that parent negatively, your child may be led to see him/herself in the same light.

5. Encourage your child to have a good relationship with your former spouse's new husband or wife. It's in your child's best interest not to feel s/he should show loyalty and love for you by disliking the stepparent your former spouse has brought into your child's life.

6. Encourage your child to talk with you about his or her feelings. It's important not to be defensive or to try to talk your child out of his/her feelings by suggesting that s/he is "wrong" or not being "fair." Just signaling your child that it's fine to talk about the difficulties is very helpful.

7. Watch for signs of depression in your child: withdrawal, excessive crying, a sad mood that lasts, irritability, loss of interest in activities that s/he normally loves, difficulty with sleeping or eating. Seeing a family counselor can be enormously helpful. Often medical insurance will help pay for it. There are also agencies that offer sliding fee scales to make professional help affordable. Your doctor can give you suggestions, or try the yellow pages under Counseling. Choose a licensed social worker or psychologist who specializes in family counseling.

8. Remember that no family is perfect. Think in terms of making problems smaller without expecting them to disappear. Family discussions about "one thing we can do to make a problem smaller and one thing we can do to make something good bigger" work well because they don't take on too much. Everyone feels hopeful when there's a positive process they know how to use.